P9-CLR-467

ABDO Publishing Company is the exclusive school and library distributor of Rabbit Ears Books.

Library bound edition 2005.

Library of Congress Cataloging-in-Publication Data

Metaxas, Eric.
Peachboy / written by Eric Metaxas ; illustrated by Jeffrey Smith.
p. cm.
"Rabbit Ears books."
Summary: Found floating on the river inside a peach by an old couple, Momotaro grows up and fights the terrible demons who have terrorized the village for years.
ISBN 1-59679-227-2
[1. Folklore—Japan.] I. Smith, Jeffrey, ill. II. Title.

PZ8.1.M518Pe 2005
398.2'0952'02—dc22
[E]

2004059647

All Rabbit Ears books are reinforced library binding
and manufactured in the United States of America.

PEACHBOY

written by Eric Metaxas
illustrated by Jeffrey Smith

RABBIT EARS BOOKS

Once upon a time in ancient Japan there lived an old woodcutter and his wife. Many years before, their children had been stolen by a band of horrible ogres. The couple had not had other children after that and had long since given up thinking about it, for they were very old.

But every now and then, as they sat on their veranda at the end of the day and watched the blue sky transformed by the orange and peach colors of the setting sun, tears would come into their eyes, and they would sigh and remember the voices of their long lost little ones and wonder what it might be like to have a child again.

Now one day, as the old woman was washing her clothes in a nearby stream, she saw a large, brilliant object that looked like a peach bobbing along in the water just beyond her. The object was so large that she knew it was not a peach and could never be one, but when at last she reached it and beheld it closely, she saw that it was a peach after all. And when she picked it up, she saw that it was nearly as large as the basket in which she carried her clothes.

So she brought the peach home and then sat on the veranda, waiting for her husband to come home. He was still a great distance off when she saw him and called out, "Ojiisan, Ojiisan! I have found a giant peach! Come quickly!"

Now the old man was carrying an exceptionally large load of wood upon his back that day, but on hearing his old wife call out to him, he hurried up the path to their home, huffing and puffing.

When he saw her sitting there on the veranda with the monumental peach, he put the wood down and rubbed his eyes, thinking that perhaps because he was so weary he was imagining things. But he soon saw that the unlikely fruit was quite real, and he marveled at it.

After they had beheld its magnificence for some time, they decided to eat it for supper.

The weary Ojiisan produced a large knife and proceeded to slice the giant object carefully in two halves. Just as he came near the middle, though, a little voice cried out. Before the old couple knew what was happening, the two halves of the vast peach fell apart, and a tiny child came out of the fruit's center and stood before them, dripping wet.

Now, of course, the old couple were quite dumbfounded, and they could only look at each other and shrug. But after a time it became clear to them that now, even at this late point in their lives, they would again know the joy of having a child all their own.

Their happiness on beholding the little child and on realizing what had befallen them in the twilight of their lives was so unspeakable that they sat and wept for many hours, and together experienced the singular sensation of not knowing what to do with their hands or feet.

The years that followed were ones of great joy for the old couple. And now, when at the end of each day they sat on the veranda watching the sun crawl under the horizon's covers for the night, the Peachboy watched it with them. And for the first time in their lives the powerful longing that came to them at this time of day found its long-deserved and proper rest.

Now as you may have heard, the Peachboy, or Momotaro as they came to call him, grew much more quickly than your average child. In fact, he grew so quickly that in only five years' time he was celebrating his fifteenth birthday. The old couple hardly knew what to make of the strange fact, but they were simple people with few expectations, and so they came to accept it as a matter of course.

One day soon thereafter, the Peachboy made an announcement to his venerable foster parents:

"It is time I go out into the wide world and prove myself as a man," he told them. "There is an island far beyond the Northeast Sea, which is inhabited by a band of hideous ogres. I must travel there and conquer them. But fear not, for I shall be victorious, and I promise to return to you when I have won back the precious plunder, which those murdering thieves have stolen over all these years."

Now Momotaro was indeed bigger and stronger than anyone they had ever seen, and his fame had spread throughout all of Japan. But the old couple had grown to love him more dearly than anything else in their lives, and the very thought of losing another dear child to the hideous ogres caused them to tremble. In the end, though, their love for the boy was so great that they were unable to deny him the desire of his heart, and so they assented.

The old man rummaged about and found a limber walking stick; a rusting iron *gunsen*, which served as a shield in warfare; and finally, a tattered old flag, which his father had given him some fifty years before, and he offered these objects to Momotaro.

The old woman ground millet seeds in the kitchen mortar, and with tears in her eyes she cooked her beloved boy a feast of dumplings over the charcoal fire. She then wrapped them up in a *furoshiki* and gave the bundle to him for his journey.

Their farewell was a long and tearful one, but finally Momotaro departed from them and set off by himself at daybreak into the wide world.

He walked and walked for what seemed many hours until finally he came into a strange country in which the colors and shapes were unlike anything he had ever seen before.

After a while he began to feel tired and lonely, so he sat down in a large field beneath a tree to rest and have a bite to eat. But when he opened his bag and smelled the millet dumplings that his dear mother had made for him with her own hands, great tears welled up in his eyes.

Just as he was finished eating, there was a terrific rustling in the bushes nearby, and suddenly a huge dog the size of a colt bounded out toward him.

"What are you doing trespassing on my land?" the dog inquired roughly, moving his head from side to side. "You'd better give me those dumplings, or I won't be responsible for my actions toward you!" And he continued to move his head from side to side, eyeing the dumplings.

"Ho, ho!" Momotaro replied. "See here, little doggie. As I remember, dogs can't even talk. How is it then that you have the audacity not only to talk but to demand of me the very dumplings that my poor mother made for me with her own hands?"

Realizing that it was indeed the Great Lord Momotaro of whom he'd heard, the insolent hound quickly changed his tune.

"You are quite right that dogs can't talk, Lord Momotaro. Quite right, indeed. What a silly notion! Please forgive me. I'll never talk again . . . although I still wouldn't mind one of those fine dumplings."

"And you shall have it," Momotaro replied. "Will you also accompany me on my journey to the island of ogres across the Northeast Sea?"

The dog said that he would and gladly agreed to be Momotaro's military retainer. He was then immediately given a dumpling as well as the high honor of carrying Lord Momotaro's walking stick, and the two of them fell in together and began walking.

They walked for miles and miles until the countryside became densely wooded. When they had grown quite tired and decided to sit down for a bite to eat, Momotaro untied the ends of the *furoshiki* containing the dumplings and immediately heard a loud screech in the tree just above them. An ancient orange ape swung down to the ground.

"Good day to you, Lord Momotaro," he said. "I've been expecting you. Word has traveled far and wide about your expedition. May I have the high honor of accompanying you?"

"The honor would be mine alone," replied Momotaro. "Please, have a dumpling."

Now the dog clearly resented the ape's intrusion into things—he had hoped to be the only one to accompany Momotaro—and as they proceeded, he and the ape snapped and bit at each other behind Momotaro's back.

As they were traveling through a moor, the dog left off bickering with the ape just long enough to flush a large pheasant out of some bushes and chase after it. The pheasant proved more than a match for the large dog, though, and could not be caught.

"You are quite a valiant fellow," Momotaro said to the bird. "We are traveling to the Isle of Death to vanquish the terrible ogres who live there. Will you do us the honor of joining our party?"

The pheasant said that he'd been born for that very purpose and agreed heartily. Momotaro then tossed up a millet dumpling, which the pheasant caught in midair and ate.

As they were traveling along, however, the strife among the animals continued until Momotaro could stand it no longer.

"Now see here," he said sternly. "We shall be quite unable to fulfill our plan if we continue to fight among ourselves. The next one of you who steps out of line shall forfeit his place among the group!"

The ape, the dog, and the pheasant all looked down at the ground sheepishly, for they deeply respected Momotaro and they were grieved that they had endangered his plan. They continued to march toward the sea, and from that day on, they were quite obedient.

Finally, after many days of marching, they came to a cliff that overlooked the great Northeast Sea. But look as they might, there was not any island to be seen.

"My dear pheasant," Momotaro pronounced solemnly, "the time has come for you to use your gift of flight. You must fly high up into the sky until you see the ogres' island."

And so the pheasant ate another millet dumpling to bolster his strength and took off into the blue sky. Higher and higher and higher he flew until they could see him no more.

In the hours that passed they constructed a ship. Then night fell, and still the pheasant did not return. Finally, early the next morning, he returned to them, completely exhausted. He explained to them that he had flown beyond the blueness of the sky itself and into a thin, clear realm untraveled by any birds.

"I had just flown through the horns of the crescent moon when I saw the island of the ogres," he explained. "It will be a long journey, but I will lead the way. Only follow me and we will prevail!"

And so Momotaro and the pheasant and the dog and the ape rode across the mountains of the waves toward their destination. Days and nights came and went as they pressed on.

At night, from the deck of the ship, they saw shooting stars arc across the heavens like wet pearls, and when the sun rose in the morning, they saw flying fish skittering among the furrows of the waves.

Word of their journey traveled far and wide beneath the water's surface, so that after a few days, a school of brilliant green dolphins rose up alongside to greet them and then leaped ahead of the boat like a military escort.

Then after some time whales appeared, and then many birds began arriving from near lands and then from distant lands. At first there were hundreds of them, and then thousands, and then more thousands. And they, too, escorted the boat, flying alongside in great multitudes, embroidering the air with song.

After many weeks the water around the boat boiled with dolphins and countless other beautiful fish, and the birds continued to come from every part of the globe, until it seemed there was not a bird or fish alive that had not come to join the fantastic procession.

They traveled along like this for many days, until the sky became so filled with music and color, and the sea with fish and spouting whales and the bright turquoise backs of the leaping

dolphins, that Momotaro thought perhaps he was in heaven and had only dreamed of his life on earth and his trip to the island of the ogres.

But one day he was watching the sun set from the deck of his ship, and as it gathered weight and began to droop slowly toward the horizon, it reminded him of a large overripe peach hanging from a branch. Then he thought of his origins and of his years among the old couple who had raised him and of his vow to destroy the ogres. And he knew that life was not a dream, and that he existed in a world that was cohabited by death, and that he was not in heaven—no, not yet—and he wept.

When he awoke, it was morning. He looked up at the horizon and then saw in the distance the tiny dot that was the Isle of Death.

Already at that distance the acrid stench of sulfur fumes burned his nostrils, and the water became a lifeless greenish color, and the fish and the dolphins and the whales and the birds fell back now, for they could go no further.

When the ship landed, Momotaro observed that the island was covered everywhere with tall plumes of yellow and greenish smoke from the sulfur springs he had heard of, and the shoreline was parched and cracked and coated with salt. There was nothing but death and silence in the air.

They trekked along in this blank landscape and saw no life. After they had walked a long while, they came to a grotesque fortress made entirely out of human bones.

"By now the ogres will have heard of our arrival," pronounced the ape. "They are perfect cowards and will try to escape into the bowels of the earth with their captives and plunder. We must hurry!"

The pheasant was quickly dispatched to report on things and soon returned. "The ogres are running about in complete panic and are indeed trying to gather up their plunder," he said.

Momotaro had a plan. In a moment the pheasant again flew up over the battlement and began calling out, "The Great Lord Momotaro has come! The Great Lord Momotaro has come!"

Then the dog ran along the walls of the fortress and barked, "The Great Lord Momotaro has come! The Great Lord Momotaro has come!"

Finally the ape clambered up to the top of the fortress wall and ran along it, shouting, "The Great Lord Momotaro has come! The Great Lord Momotaro has come!"

On hearing this news, the ogres gnashed their teeth and pulled their horns out. Then, in their fear and confusion, they began attacking each other. Finally, the din of their wailing and panic was so great that the very walls of the fortress itself began to crumble.

As the walls fell, Momotaro immediately climbed over the rubble. On seeing him, the ogres shrieked and dropped all of the plunder they were carrying in order to escape into the center of the fortress. Momotaro and his companions went quickly after them.

But just as they entered the innermost chamber of the fortress, they saw the last ogre disappear into a hole that led to the bowels of the earth. Quickly, Momotaro gave the dog his iron *gunsen* and climbed in after them, while his friends waited anxiously.

As they were waiting, though, a great earthquake shook the entire island. It was so powerful that the ape, the dog and the pheasant all fell to the ground, and the fortress around them began to crumble. When it had finally stopped, they were quiet, for they were all convinced that Momotaro had met his end.

But just as they were about to leave, they heard a noise coming from inside the hole. Momotaro was alive! And as he emerged from the hole, they saw that he was followed by a huge train of the ogres' captives, all the people who had been stolen as children and held prisoner all these years.

When all the people had finally come out, Momotaro picked up a huge rock, and with it, he sealed the entrance to the bowels of the earth forever.

Now, because of the great earthquake, the sulfur springs around the island had been instantly transformed into gushing fountains of water that flowed everywhere. And now all of the soil that had been formerly parched and cracked erupted with trees and green plants and flowers. Even the horrible smell of sulfur and fear that was in the air evaporated and was eclipsed by the powerful and beautiful fragrance of peach blossoms.

On seeing this, everyone sang out in joy. Then they marched back to Momotaro's ship with the ogres' plunder, and accompanied by the birds and the fish and the whales and the leaping dolphins, they began the long journey home, back into the setting sun.